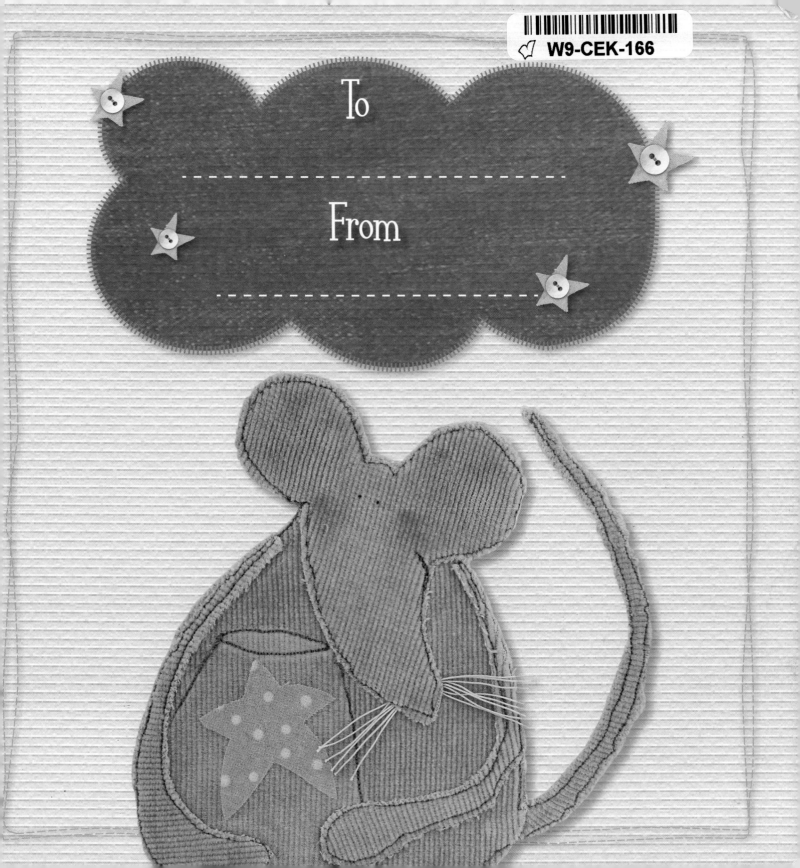

To

From

Twinkle Twinkle Little Star

Kate Toms

make
believe
ideas

Twinkle, twinkle,

little **star**,

how I wonder

what **you** are,

I'd love to catch you in my net . . .

and keep you as a special pet!

Twinkle, twinkle,
little **star**,
I do so **wonder** what **you** are.

When **snuggled** up in bed at night,

cozy, **warm**, and **tucked** up tight,

I dream that I can fly a rocket . . .

5 4 3 2

and gather stardust in my pocket.

Twinkle, twinkle, little **star**, how I wonder what **you** are.

Does a **man** live on the **moon**?

Wait for me!

And did he see the dish and spoon?

And if the **moon**

Yummy!

is made of **cheese**,

Twinkle, twinkle, little star,

what do you see from afar?

Hello!

¡Hola!

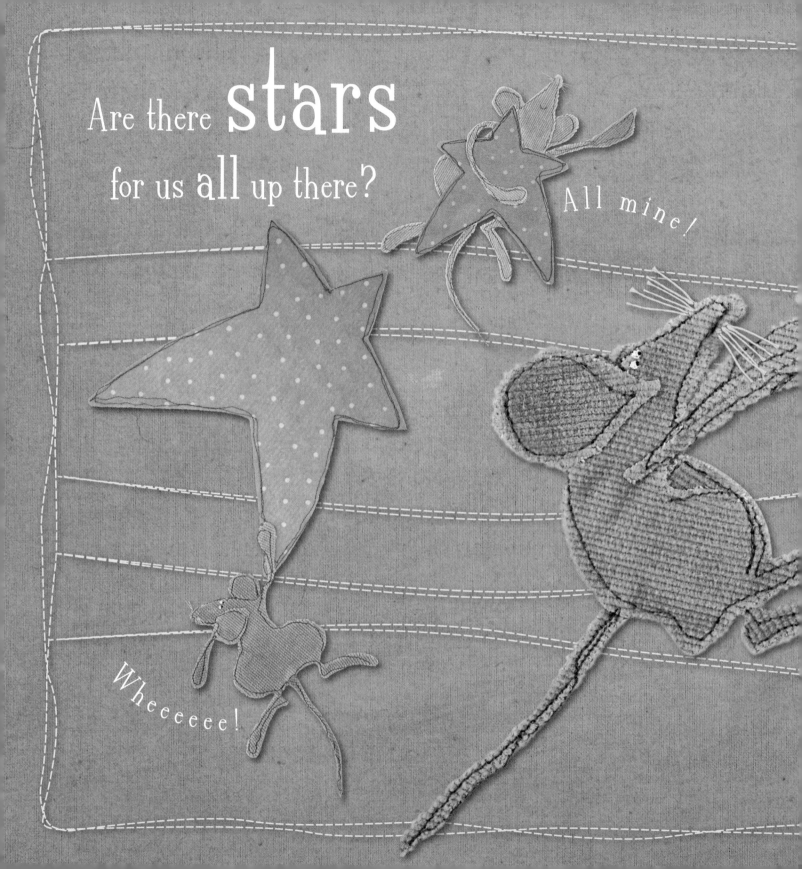

Are there **stars** for us **all** up there?

All mine!

Wheeeeee!

Jump!

Or do some folks have to **share?**

Twinkle, twinkle, little star,
how I wonder
what you are!

When the sky
grows dark at night,
I wish and wish
with all my might,

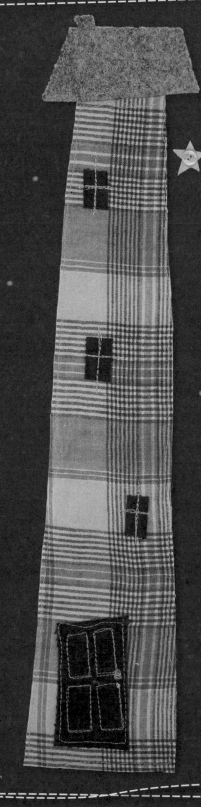

that you would look down
on my **house**,
and grant one thing
for this small **mouse**.

I want to be a
star like you,

Wheeeeeeeee!

and see the world the way you do.

Twinkle, twinkle, little star,
how I wonder what you are.

When it's time to climb the stairs,

to **brush** my **teeth**
and say my **prayers,**

through my **window,** I can see
that you are **smiling** down on me.

Twinkle, twinkle, little **star**, how I wonder what **you** are,